To my mother, who showed me the world

First published 2003 by Walker Books Ltd, 87 Vauxhall Walk, London SE11 5HJ

1 2 3 4 5 6 7 8 9 10

This book has been typeset in Calligraphic Bold

Printed in Hong Kong

British Library Cataloguing in Publication Data: a catalogue record for this book is available from the British Library

ISBN 0-7445-9281-X

Hello World

Michael Foreman

WALKER BOOKS
AND SUBSIDIARIES
LONDON • BOSTON • SYDNEY

"Wake up, Baby. Let's go and see the world."

"Listen, the birds are singing,
'Wake up, wake up.'"

“Hello, kittens. Come and see the world with us.”

"Will there be trees to climb?"

"Yes, and much much more."

"Hello, puppies.
Come and see the world."
"Will there be fields to run in?"
"Yes, run along
with us."

"Hello, Mrs Frog. We're off to see the world."

"Will there be a warm rock to lie on?"

"Yes, come and see."

"Hello, Mrs
Duck. We're off
to see the world."

"Will there be a pond for me and my ducklings?"

"Yes, a pond and more besides."

"We'll waddle along with you, then."

"Hello, Mrs Hen.
Come with
us and see
the world."

"Will there be corn to peck?"

"Yes, come and bring your chicks."

"Follow us, follow us;
we're off to see the world."

And they saw a pond
with warm rocks to lie on.

And they saw
trees to climb.

And they saw fields of flowers and stacks of corn.

And they loved it all.

"Is there more?"

"Yes, come and see."

It was wonderful.

looking back at them.